Betsy-Tacy

Betsy-Tacy

Maud Hart Lovelace

Illustrated by *Lois Lenski*

■ HarperTrophy®
An Imprint of HarperCollinsPublishers

Betsy-Tacy
Copyright © 1940 by Maud Hart Lovelace
Copyright renewed 1968 by Maud Hart Lovelace
Author note from *Minnesota Writes* and reproduced with permission.
Copyright © 1961 by Instructional Fair • TS Denison
"Maud Hart Lovelace and Her World" (adapted from *The Betsy-Tacy Companion:
A Biography of Maud Hart Lovelace* by Sharla Scannell Whalen)
Copyright © 2000 by HarperCollins Publishers

Library of Congress catalog card number: 40-30965
ISBN 978-0-06-440096-1
First published in hardcover by Thomas Y. Crowell Company in 1940
First Harper Trophy edition, 1979
Revised Harper Trophy edition, 2007
13 LP/RRDH 40 39 38 37 36 35 34

To
*B*ICK *and* M*ERIAN*

Contents

Author's Note

I cannot remember back to a year in which I did not consider myself to be a writer, and the younger I was the bigger the capital "W." Back in Mankato I wrote stories in notebooks and illustrated them with pictures cut from magazines. When I was ten my father, I hope at not too great expense, had printed a booklet of my earliest rhymes. Soon after I started bombarding the magazines and sold my first story when I was eighteen.

For a long time now I have been happily absorbed in a succession of books for children, chiefly the Betsy-Tacy series. I began these by pure accident. Earlier, for many years, I wrote historical novels and there was a time when I would have told you I was unlikely ever to write anything else. The field delighted me. Especially, I loved the research involved.

I was well into my fourth novel when our daughter Merian was born—quite unexpectedly, because we had been married fourteen years. I finished that novel and wrote two more in collaboration with my husband. But I found myself less and less interested in inventing plots for adult readers. As Merian grew old enough to listen to stories, I loved to tell them to her and I found that most of them centered about my own happy childhood in Mankato. By the time she was seven, and my writer's (now a small "w") conscience was upbraiding me because I had not done a book for several years, I saw suddenly that I could make a book of the stories I was telling her.

The first of the Betsy-Tacy books resulted and ever since then I have written stories for children, most of them about Betsy who is, in some measure, myself. The Ray family is plainly the Hart family. I meet grandfathers now who tell me that they still remember my father's onion sandwiches. It is a great joy to me to have that dear family between book covers.

I must make clear that these are books of fiction. Plots for them have been invented freely. But many—although not all—of the characters are based on real people.

This situation led me into a new kind of research. Letters began to fly. "Tacy," "Tib," "Carney," and other close friends answered lists of questions from me about themselves and our doings when we were young. They drew diagrams of Mankato streets. (Mankato is the Deep Valley of the stories.) They sent old photographs of themselves and their relatives and their houses which Lois Lenski and Vera Neville enjoyed embodying in their delightful pictures. I dived into my own diaries and kodak books and memory books, while the New York Public Library—and later the Claremont libraries—helped out with old newspapers, old fashion magazines, collections of old popular songs, and Sears and Roebuck catalogues.

As our daughter grew up, so did Betsy, and there are now ten mainline Betsy-Tacy stories and three more in which Betsy appears. The letters from children which began with *Betsy-Tacy* flow into our mailbox and are a constant inducement to continue writing juvenile books.

Maud Lovelace

1961

There was a time when meadow, grove, and stream,
The earth, and every common sight,
  To me did seem
Apparell'd in celestial light,
The glory and the freshness of a dream . . .

—WILLIAM WORDSWORTH

1

Betsy Meets Tacy

IT WAS difficult, later, to think of a time when Betsy and Tacy had not been friends. Hill Street came to regard them almost as one person. Betsy's brown braids went with Tacy's red curls, Betsy's plump legs with Tacy's spindly ones, to school and from school, up hill and down, on errands and in play. So that when Tacy had the mumps and Betsy was obliged to make her journeys alone, saucy boys teased her: "Where's the cheese, apple pie?" "Where's your mush, milk?" As though she didn't feel lonesome enough already! And Hill Street knew when Sunday came, even without listening to the rolling bells, for Betsy Ray and Tacy Kelly (whose parents attended different churches), set off down Hill Street separately, looking uncomfortable and strange.

But on this March afternoon, a month before Betsy's fifth birthday, they did not know each other. They had not even seen each other, unless Betsy had glimpsed Tacy, without knowing her for Tacy, among the children of assorted sizes moving into the house across the street. Betsy had been kept in because of bad weather, and all day she had sat with her nose pasted to the pane. It was exciting beyond words to have a family with children moving into that house.

Hill Street was rightfully named. It ran straight up into a green hill and stopped. The name of the town was Deep Valley, and a town named Deep Valley naturally had plenty of hills. Betsy's house, a small yellow cottage, was the last house on her side of Hill Street, and the rambling white house opposite was the last house on that side. So of course it was very important. And it had been empty ever since Betsy could remember.

"I hope whoever moves in will have children," Betsy's mother had said.

"Well, for Pete's sake!" said Betsy's father. "Hill Street is so full of children now that Old Mag has to watch out where she puts her feet down."

"I know," said Betsy's mother. "There are plenty of children for Julia." (Julia was Betsy's sister, eight years old.) "And there are dozens of babies. But there isn't one little girl just Betsy's age. And that's what I'm hoping will come to the house across the street."

That was what Betsy hoped, too. And that was what she had been watching for all day as she sat at the dining room window. She was certain there must be such a little girl. There were girls of almost every size and boys to match, milling about the moving dray and in and out of the house. But she wasn't sure. She hadn't absolutely seen one.

She had watched all day, and now the dining room was getting dark. Julia had stopped practicing her music lesson, and Mrs. Ray had lighted the lamp in the kitchen.

The March snow lay cold and dirty outside the window, but the wind had died down, and the western sky, behind the house opposite, was stained with red.

The furniture had all been carried in, and the dray was gone. A light was shining in the house. Suddenly the front door opened, and a little girl ran out. She wore a hood beneath which long red ringlets spattered out above her coat. Her legs in their long black stockings were thin.

It was Tacy, although Betsy did not know it!

She ran first to the hitching block, and bounced there on her toes a minute, looking up at the sky and all around. Then she ran up the road to the point where it ended on the hill. Some long-gone person had placed a bench there. It commanded the view down Hill Street. The little girl climbed up on this bench and looked intently into the dusk.

"I know just how she feels," thought Betsy with a throb. "This is her new home. She wants to see what it's like." She ran to her mother.

"Mamma!" she cried. "There's the little girl my age. Please let me go out! Just a minute! Please!"

Mrs. Ray was moved by the entreaty. She looked out at the colored sky.

"It does seem to be clearing up," she said. "But you could only stay a minute. Do you want to go to the bother of putting on your things . . ."

"Oh, yes, yes!"

"Overshoes and mittens and everything?"

"Yes, really!"

Betsy flew to the closet, but she could not find her pussy hood. The mittens were twisted on the string inside her coat.

"Mamma! Help me! Please! She'll be gone."

"Help her, Julia," called Betsy's mother, and Julia helped, and at last the pussy hood was tied, and the coat buttoned, and the overshoes buckled, and the mittens pulled on.

Outside the air was fresh and cold. The street lamp had been lighted. It was exciting just to be out at this hour, even without the prospect of meeting the new little girl. But the new little girl still stood on the bench looking down the street.

Betsy ran toward her. She ran on the sidewalk as far as it went. Then she took to the frozen rutty road, and she had almost reached the bench when the little girl saw her.

"Hello!" called Betsy. "What's your name?"

The other child made no answer. She jumped off the bench.

"Don't go!" cried Betsy. "I'm coming."

But the other child without a word began to run. She brushed past Betsy on her headlong flight down the hill. She ran like a frightened rabbit, and Betsy ran in pursuit.

"Wait! Wait!" Betsy panted as she ran. But the new child would not stop. On fleet, black-stockinged legs she ran, faster than Betsy could follow.

"Wait! Wait!" pleaded Betsy but the child did not turn her head. She gained her own lawn, floundered through the snow to her house.

The entrance to her house was through a storm shed. She ran into this and banged the door. The door had a pane of glass in the front, and through that pane she stared fearfully at Betsy.

Betsy stood still, winking back tears, a mittened finger in her mouth. At last she turned and trudged slowly back through the snowy dark to her house.

She had almost reached her porch when the door of the storm shed opened. The new little girl stuck out her head.

"Tacy!" she shouted.

"You needn't call names!" Betsy shouted back. Tacy was shouting her own name, really. But it was such an odd one, Betsy didn't understand.

She trudged on into the house.

The lamp hanging over the dining room table was lighted now. A delicious smell of fried potatoes floated from the kitchen. "Well," her mother called out cheerfully. "Did you get acquainted?"

"What's her name?" asked Julia.

"I don't know. I don't like her. I'm mad at her," said Betsy. It was all she could do not to cry.

That was as near as Betsy and Tacy ever came to

a quarrel. And of course it didn't count. For they weren't friends yet.

They began to be friends next month, in April, at Betsy's birthday party.

2

Betsy's Birthday Party

HE TIME in between was lost because of bad weather. It was filled with snowing and blowing, raining and sleeting. It seemed as though spring never would come. But up in the hills pasque flowers were lifting their purple heads; and down in the valley beside the frozen river, the willow twigs were yellow. Birds were back from the south, shivering red-winged blackbirds and bluebirds and robins. Betsy and Tacy peeped out their windows at them, and if they saw each other they made faces and pulled down the blinds.

However, when it came time to make out the list for Betsy's birthday party, Betsy's mother included Tacy.

"Of course we'll invite the little girl from across the street," she said. And she spoke to Julia. "Will you find out what her name is?"

For Julia, who was eight years old and went to school, was acquainted now with Tacy's older sister. Katie was her name; she was eight, too.

Julia came home next day at noon and said, "Her name is Tacy."

"Tacy!" said Betsy. "Tacy!"

She felt herself growing warm. She knew then for the first time that Tacy hadn't been calling names when she put her head around the storm shed door, but had meant to say that she wanted to be friends after all.

"It's an odd name," said Mrs. Ray. "What does it stand for?"

"Anastacia. She's Anna Anastacia."

So Mrs. Ray wrote out the invitation, inviting Tacy to Betsy's birthday party. She invited Katie, too, to be company for Julia. She invited fifteen boys and girls in all.

"I hope to goodness it will be nice weather," said Betsy's mother. "Then they can play out of doors."

For the Ray house was small. But the sloping lawn was big, with maples and a butternut tree in front of the house, and behind it fruit trees and berry bushes and a garden, and Old Mag's barn, and the shed where the carriage was kept.

It would be much more fun if they could play out of doors, Betsy thought.

She was excited about the party, for she had never had one before. And she was to wear her first silk dress. It was checked tan and pink, with lace around the neck and sleeves. Her mother had promised to take her hair out of braids for the party. She had promised to dress it in curls.

Sure enough, on the night before the party, after Julia and Betsy had had their baths in the tub set out before the kitchen fire, Betsy's hair was rolled up on rags. There were curl-making bumps all over her head. And either because of the bumps or because the party was getting so near, Betsy could hardly sleep at all. She would wake up and think, "There's going to be ice cream!" And then she'd go to sleep again. And then she'd wake up and think, "I wonder if Tacy will come." And so it went, all night long. When she woke up finally it was morning, and the sun was shining so brightly that it had quite dried off the lawn, which had been free of snow for several days.

Betsy flew downstairs to breakfast.

"Dear me," said her father, shaking his head when he saw her. "Betsy can't have a party. She's sick. Look how red her cheeks are! Look at those bumps that have come out on her head."

Betsy's father loved to joke. Of course there were bumps on her head, because the curls hadn't been unwrapped. They weren't unwrapped for hours, not until almost time for the party. Betsy's hair didn't take kindly to curls.

But her hair was good and curly when the rags were removed. It stood out in a soft brown fluff about her face, which was round with very red cheeks and a smile which showed teeth parted in the middle.

"When Betsy is happy," her mother said, "she is happier than anyone else in the world." Then she added, "And she's almost always happy."

She was happy today . . . although she had little shivers inside her for fear that Tacy wouldn't come. The silk dress rustled beautifully over two starched petticoats which were buttoned to a muslin under-waist over woolen underwear. The legs of the underwear were folded tightly under her white party stockings and into the tops of her shoes. They made her legs look even chunkier than they were. She and Julia had hoped that their winter underwear would come off for the party. But their mother had said, "In April? Certainly not!"

At one minute after half-past two, the children started coming. Each one brought a birthday present which he gave to Betsy at the door. Each one said, "Happy birthday!" and Betsy said, "Thank you!" And one little boy who was named Tom said, "Let'th thppeak pietheth." (He meant to say, "Let's speak pieces," but he couldn't, because he had lost two teeth and the new ones weren't in yet.)

Betsy kept waiting for Tacy to come. At last she saw her crossing the street, hanging on to Katie's hand. Tacy held her head down, so that her long red ringlets almost covered her face. You could hardly see what she looked like.

She handed Betsy a package, looking down all the while. The present was a little glass pitcher with a gold painted rim. She wouldn't look up when Betsy thanked her. She wouldn't say, "Happy birthday!"

"She's bashful," Katie explained.

She certainly was bashful. She hung on to Katie's hand as though she were afraid she would be drowned if she let go. She wouldn't join in any of the games. She wouldn't even try to pin the tail on the donkey.

The sun shone warmly so that they could play their games on the lawn. Betsy's mother gave prizes. To please the little boy named Tom she let them all speak pieces. He knew a piece . . . that was why he had been so anxious to have them spoken.

"Twinkle, twinkle, little thtar," he said, his eyes shining like big brown stars.

But all the while Tacy kept her head snuggled against Katie's arm.

At last Julia formed the children in a line. Betsy's mother would play a march on the piano, she explained. Betsy, because she was the birthday child, could choose a partner and lead the line. They would march into the house for their refreshments.

The music started, and when Tacy heard the music she tossed back her curls a little. Betsy was sorry she had made that mistake about saying, "Don't call names!" so she chose Tacy for her partner. And Betsy and Tacy took hold of hands and marched at the head of the line.

They marched around and around the house and in and out of the parlor and the back parlor. Betsy's mother loved to play the piano; she came down hard and joyously on the keys. Every once in a while Tacy would look at Betsy sidewise through her curls. Her bright blue eyes were dancing in her little freckled face, as though to say, "Isn't this fun?" They marched and they marched, and at last they were told to lead the way to the dining room. There the cake was shining with all its five candles, and a dish of ice cream was set out for every child.

Betsy kept hold of Tacy's hand, and they sat down side by side. From that time on, at almost every party, you found Betsy and Tacy side by side.

Betsy was given beautiful presents at that fifth birthday party. Besides the little glass pitcher, she got colored cups and saucers, a small silk handkerchief embroidered with forget-me-nots, pencils and puzzles and balls. But the nicest present she received was not the usual kind of present. It was the present of a friend. It was Tacy.

3
Supper on the Hill

THAT SUMMER they started having picnics. At first the picnics were not real
picnics; not the kind you take out in a basket. Betsy's father, serving the plates at the head of
the table, would fill Betsy's plate with scrambled
eggs and bread and butter and strawberries, or
whatever they had for supper. Tacy's father would
do the same. Holding the plate in one hand and a

glass of milk in the other, each little girl would walk carefully out of her house and down the porch steps and out to the middle of the road. Then they would walk up the hill to that bench where Tacy had stood the first night she came. And there they would eat supper together.

Betsy always liked what she saw on Tacy's plate. In particular she liked the fresh unfrosted cake which Tacy's mother often stirred up for supper for her big family. Tacy knew that Betsy liked that cake, and she always divided her piece. And if baked beans or corn bread or something that Tacy liked lay on Betsy's plate, Betsy divided that too.

While they ate they watched the sun setting behind Tacy's house. Sometimes the west showed clouds like tiny pink feathers; sometimes it showed purple mountains and green lakes; sometimes the clouds were scarlet with gold around the edges. Betsy liked to make up stories, so she made up stories about the sunset. When she couldn't think what to say next, Tacy helped her.

Betsy always put herself and Tacy in the stories. Like this:

One night two little girls named Betsy and Tacy were eating their supper on the hill. The hill was covered with flowers. They smelled sweet and were pink like the sky. The sky was covered with little pink feathers.

"I wish," said Tacy, "that I had a feather for my hat."

"Do you really?" asked Betsy.

"Certainly I do," said Tacy.

"I'll get you one," said Betsy.

She stood up on the bench. They were through eating their suppers and had put their plates down in the grass. Betsy stood up on the bench and reached her hand out for a feather.

Tacy said, "You can't reach that feather. It's way over our house."

Betsy said, "I can so."

She reached and she reached; and the first thing she knew one of the feathers had come near enough for her to touch it. But when she took hold of it, instead of coming down, it began pulling her up.

Tacy saw what was happening, and she took hold of Betsy's feet. She was just in time too. In another minute Betsy would have been gone. Up, up, up they went on the feather into the sky.

They floated over Tacy's house. The smoke was coming out of the chimney where her mother had cooked supper. Far below were Tacy's pump and barn and buggy shed. They looked strange and small.

Betsy and Tacy could see Betsy's house too. They could look all the way down Hill Street. They could see Mr. Williams milking his cow. And Mr. Benson driving home late to supper.

Betsy said, "Wouldn't our fathers and mothers be surprised, if they could look up here and see us sitting on a feather?" For by this time they had climbed up on the feather and were sitting on it side by side. They put their arms around each other so that they wouldn't fall. It was fun sitting up there.

"I wish Julia and Katie could see us," said Tacy. Julia and Katie were like most big sisters. They were bossy. Of course they were eight, but even if they were eight, they weren't so smart. They didn't know how to float off on a feather like Betsy and Tacy were doing.

"We'd better not let anyone see us, though," Betsy decided. "They'd think it was dangerous. They wouldn't let us do it again, and I'd like to do it every night."

"So would I," said Tacy. "Tomorrow night, let's float down over the town and see Front Street where the stores are."

"And the river," said Betsy.

"And the park," said Tacy. "Page Park with the white fence around it and the picnic benches and the swings."

"We may even go there to eat our supper some night," Betsy said. "Let's go some night when your mother has baked cake."

"Do you suppose we could hold on to our plates?" asked Tacy. "When we were riding on this feather?"

"We'd have to hold tight," Betsy said, and they looked down. It made them dizzy to look down, they were so high up.

Tacy began to laugh. "We'd have to be careful not to spill our milk," she said.

"We might spill our milk on Julia and Katie," Betsy cried.

"I wouldn't care if we did."

"It would make them mad, though."

And at the thought of spilling milk on Julia and Katie and making them mad, they laughed so hard that they tipped their feather over. It went over quick like a paper boat, and they started falling, falling, falling. But they didn't fall too fast. It was delicious the way they fell . . . like a swallow sinking down, down, down . . . to the very bench where they had been sitting.

Only now the sunset had dimmed a little and the grass was cold with dew and down in their door-yards Betsy's mother and one or two of Tacy's brothers and sisters were calling, "Betsy!" "Tacy!" "Betsy!" "Tacy!"

Betsy and Tacy looked at each other with shining eyes.

"Don't forget it's a secret," Betsy said, "that we can go floating off whenever we like."

"I won't forget," said Tacy.

"Tomorrow night we'd better bring jackets, if we're going down to Front Street. I felt a little cold sitting up on that feather, didn't you?"

"Yes," said Tacy, wriggling her bare toes. "I wished I was wearing my shoes."

"Betsy!" called Betsy's mother.

"Tacy!" called four or five of Tacy's brothers and sisters.

"We're coming," called Betsy and Tacy, and they picked up their plates and glasses and came slowly down the hill.

That was the kind of picnic they went on at first. Later, when they grew older, they packed their picnics in baskets.

4
The Piano Box

BETSY AND Tacy soon had places which belonged to them. The bench on the hill was the first one. The second one, and the dearest for several years, was the piano box. This was their headquarters, their playhouse, the center of all their games.

It stood behind Betsy's house, for it had brought that same piano on which Julia practiced her music

lesson and which Betsy's mother had played for
Betsy's party. It was tall enough to hold a piano; so
of course it was tall enough to hold Betsy and Tacy.
It wasn't so wide as it was tall; they had to squeeze
to get in. But by squeezing just a little, they could
get in and sit down.

Julia and Katie couldn't come in unless they were
invited. This was Betsy's and Tacy's private corner.
Betsy's mother was a great believer in people having
private corners, and the piano box was plainly
meant to belong to Betsy and Tacy, for it fitted them
so snugly. They decorated the walls with pictures
cut from magazines. Tacy's mother gave them a bit
of rug for the floor. They kept their treasures of
stones and moss in a shoe box in one corner.

One side of the piano box was open. As Betsy
and Tacy sat in their retreat they had a pleasant
view. They looked into the back yard maple,
through the garden and the little grove of fruit
trees, past the barn and buggy shed, up to the Big
Hill. This was not the hill where the picnic bench
stood. That was the little hill which ended Hill
Street. Hill Street ran north and south, but the road
which climbed the Big Hill ran east and west. At the
top stood a white house, and the sun rose behind it
in the morning.

Sitting in their piano box one day, Betsy and Tacy

looked at the Big Hill. Neither of them had ever climbed it. Julia and Katie climbed it whenever they pleased.

"I think," said Betsy, "that it's time we climbed that hill." So they ran and asked their mothers.

Betsy's mother was canning strawberries. "All right," she said. "But be sure to come when I call."

"All right," said Tacy's mother. "But it's almost dinner time."

Betsy and Tacy took hold of hands and started to climb.

The road ran straight to the white house and the deep blue summer sky. The dust of the road was soft to their bare feet. The sun shone warmly on Betsy's braids and on Tacy's bright red curls.

At first they passed only Betsy's house and her

garden and orchard and barn. They had gone that far before. Then they came to a ridge where wild roses bloomed in June. They had gone that far, picking roses. But at last each step took them farther into an unknown country.

The roadside was crowded with mid-summer flowers . . . big white daisies and small fringed daisies, brown-eyed Susans and Queen Anne's lace. On one side of the road, the hill was open. On the other it was fenced, with a wire fence which enclosed a cow pasture. A brindle cow was sleeping under a scrub oak tree.

"Just think!" said Betsy. "We don't even know whose cow pasture that is."

"We don't even know whose cow that is," said Tacy. "Of course it *might* be Mr. Williams' cow."

"Oh, no," said Betsy. "We've come too far for that."

They plodded on again.

The sun seemed warmer and warmer. The dust began to pull at their feet. They turned and looked back. They could look down now on the roofs of their homes, almost as they had done the night they rode the feather.

"We've come a dreadful way," said Tacy. "If we were sitting in our piano box, we could see ourselves up here."

"We would wonder who were those two children climbing the Big Hill."

"Maybe we ought to stop," said Tacy.

"Let's go just a little farther," Betsy said. But in a moment she pointed to a fat thorn apple tree on the

unfenced side of the road. "That would be a nice place to stop," she suggested. And they stopped.

Under the thorn apple tree was a deep, soft nest of grass. The two little girls sat down and drew their knees into their arms. They could see farther now than the treetops of Hill Street. They could see the roof of the big red schoolhouse where Julia and Katie went to school.

A squirrel whisked down the tree to look at them. A phoebe sang, "Phoebe! Phoebe!" over and over again. A hornet buzzed in the noonday heat, but did not come too near.

"Let's live up here," Betsy said suddenly.

Tacy started. "You mean all the time?"

"All the time. Sleep here and everything."

"Just you and me?" Tacy asked.

"I think it would be fun," said Betsy. She jumped up and found a broken branch. "This is the front of our house," she said, laying it down.

Tacy brought a second branch and laid it so that the two ends left a space between. "This is our front door," she said.

"This is our parlor," said Betsy. "Where this stone is. Company can sit on the stone."

"And this is our bedroom," said Tacy. "If your mother will let us have her big brown shawl to sleep on, my mother will give us a pillow, I think."

They worked busily, making their house.

"But Betsy," said Tacy after a time. "What will we have to eat?"

Betsy looked thoughtfully about her. "Why, we'll milk the cow," she said.

"Do you think we could?"

"'Course we could. You hold him and I'll milk him."

"All right," said Tacy. "Only not just yet. I'm not hungry yet."

Betsy rolled her eyes upward. "We can have thorn apples too," she said.

"That's right," said Tacy happily. "We can have thorn apple pie."

They started picking thorn apples. But after a

moment Betsy interrupted the task.

"And I like eggs," she said.

Something firm and determined in her tone made Tacy look around hurriedly. Betsy was looking at a hen. It was a red hen with a red glittery breast. It had wandered up the hill from some back yard in Hill Street, perhaps. Or down the hill from the big white house. Betsy and Tacy could not tell. But Betsy was looking at the hen so firmly, there was no mistaking her intention.

"We'll catch that hen," said Betsy, "and keep him in a box. And whenever we get hungry he can lay us an egg."

"That will be fine," said Tacy.

They began to hunt for a box.

With great good fortune they found one. It was broken and old and water-soaked, but it was a box. It would hold a hen.

"Now," said Betsy, "we have to catch him. I'll say, 'Here chickabiddie, chickabiddie! Here chickabiddie, chickabiddie!' like I've heard my Uncle Edward do, and when he comes right up to my hand, you grab him."

"All right," said Tacy.

So Betsy called, "Here chickabiddie, chickabiddie! Here chickabiddie, chickabiddie!" just as she had heard her Uncle Edward do. And she called so

well and made such inviting motions with her hand (as though she were scattering feed) that the hen came running toward her. And Tacy swooped down on it with two thin arms and Betsy bundled it up in two plump ones. Somehow, although it flapped and clawed, they got it into the box.

But the hen was very angry. It glared at them with furious little eyes and opened and shut its sharp little beak and made the most horrid, terrifying squawks.

"Lay an egg, chickabiddie! Lay an egg, chickabiddie!" said Betsy over and over.

But the hen didn't lay a single egg.

About this time voices rose from Hill Street.

"Betsy!" "Tacy!" "Betsy!" "Tacy!" One voice added, "Dinner's ready."

"I don't believe he's going to lay an egg," said Tacy.

"Neither do I," said Betsy. "He isn't trained yet."

"Maybe," said Tacy, "our piano box is a nicer place to live after all."

Betsy thought it over. The hen kept making that horrid, squawking sound. Probably there would be strawberry jam for dinner, left over from what went into the jars. And the piano box was a beautiful place.

"Our piano box," she agreed, jumping up, "has a roof for when it rains."

So they ran down the Big Hill.

"We climbed the Big Hill," they shouted joyously to Julia and Katie who had been doing the calling.

"Pooh! We climb it often," Julia and Katie said.

5
The First Day of School

WHEN SEPTEMBER came, Betsy and Tacy started going to school. Julia took Betsy and Katie took Tacy, on the opening day. Betsy's mother came out on the steps of the little yellow house to wave good-by, and Tacy's mother came out on her steps, too, along with Tacy's brother Paul and Bee, the baby, who weren't old enough yet to go to school.

Betsy was beaming all over her round rosy face. Her tightly braided pigtails, with new red ribbons

on the ends, stuck out behind her ears. She wore a new plaid dress which her mother had made, and new shoes which felt stiff and queer.

Tacy's mother had brushed the ringlets over her finger 'til they shone. They hung as neat as sausages down Tacy's back. Tacy had a new dress, too; navy blue, it was, because she had red hair. But where Betsy was beaming, Tacy was frowning. She held her head down and dragged from Katie's hand.

She was bashful; that was the trouble. Betsy had almost forgotten how bashful Tacy could be. Tacy wasn't bashful with Betsy any more, but she was very bashful starting to school. "She'll get over it," said Katie, and they set off down Hill Street. The maples were beginning to turn yellow but the air was soft and warm. It smelled of the smoke from Grandpa Williams' bonfire.

"We're going to school, Grandpa Williams," Betsy called to him.

"That's fine," said Grandpa Williams.

Tacy said nothing.

They went down Hill Street to the vacant lot. It was knee deep with goldenrod and asters. It would have been fun to stop and play there, if they hadn't been going to school. But they cut through by a little path and came out on Pleasant Street.

There on the corner on a big green lawn stood a chocolate-colored house. It had porches all around it, a tower on the side, and a pane of colored glass over the front door. It was a beautiful house but they had no time to look at it. They were busy going to school.

They crossed the street and turned the corner and came to a little store.

"That's Mrs. Chubbock's store," Julia explained. "That's where you go to buy gum drops and chocolate men if anyone's given you a penny."

"I wish that someone had given me a penny. Don't you, Tacy?" Betsy asked.

Tacy didn't answer.

Just beyond Mrs. Chubbock's store, they came to the school yard. They came first to the boys' yard, a big sandy yard with one tree. On the other side of the schoolhouse was the girls' yard which looked much the same. But the girls' yard had more trees. The schoolhouse was built of red brick trimmed with yellow stone. A steep flight of steps led up to the door.

At the top of the steps stood a boy, holding a big bell. When he rang that bell, Julia explained, it was time for school to begin.

"Oh, oh!" said Betsy. "I wish that I could be the one to ring the bell. Don't you, Tacy?"

Tacy didn't say a word.

The girls playing in the school yard came crowding around Julia and Katie to see their little sisters. Tacy shook her long red curls over her face. Between the curls her face was as red as a beet. She wouldn't look up.

She didn't look up until the boy at the head of the steps began to ring the bell. Ding, dong, ding, dong, went the bell. Tacy jumped like a scared rabbit and pulled at Katie's hand. She pulled away from the schoolhouse because she didn't want to go in. But

Katie was stronger than Tacy; besides, she was the kind of person who never gave up. So she pulled harder than Tacy and got her to the Baby Room door.

Julia had already taken Betsy to the door, and had said to Miss Dalton, the teacher: "This is my little sister Betsy."

Now Katie said, "This is my little sister Tacy." And she added, "She's very bashful."

"Never mind," said Miss Dalton, smiling brightly. "I'll take care of that. I'll put her right by me." And she placed a little chair beside her desk and put Tacy into that.

Tacy didn't like it. Betsy could tell from the way she scrunched down and hid herself beneath her curls. She liked it less than ever when Betsy was put far away at a regular desk in one of the rows of desks which filled the room. But Miss Dalton was too busy to notice; Julia and Katie went out; the door closed, and school began.

If it hadn't been for Tacy's looking so forlorn, Betsy would have liked school. The windows were hung with chains made from shiny paper. On the blackboard was a calendar for the month of September drawn with colored chalk. And Miss Dalton was pretty; she looked like a canary. But it was hard for Betsy to be happy with Tacy such a picture of woe.

Instead of looking better, Tacy looked worse and worse. She gazed at Betsy with pleading eyes, and her face was screwed up as though she were going to cry.

"She's going to cry," someone whispered in Betsy's ear. It was the little boy named Tom.

"Oh!" cried Betsy. "You've got your teeth." She knew because now he said "s" as well as she did. Besides, she could see them, two brand-new teeth, right in the front of his mouth.

"Yes, I got them young," said Tom.

He sat at the desk behind Betsy's.

Betsy was glad when recess time came. They formed in two lines and marched out of the room and through the front door and down the stairs. The girls skipped off to the playground at the left, the boys to the one at the right. Now, thought Betsy, she would find Tacy and tell her not to be bashful. But when she looked about for Tacy, Tacy was nowhere to be seen.

Betsy ran to the sidewalk and looked down the street. Flying red ringlets and twinkling thin black legs were almost out of sight.

"Stop, Tacy! Stop!" cried Betsy. She ran in pursuit. But it was no use. Tacy could always run faster than Betsy. She ran faster now. At last, however, she slowed down so that Betsy could catch up.

They had reached Mrs. Chubbock's store.

"Tacy!" cried Betsy. "We're not supposed to leave the yard."

"I'm going home," said Tacy. She was crying.

"But you can't. It's not allowed."

Tacy only cried.

She cried harder than Betsy had ever seen her cry. She wrinkled up her little freckled face. Tears ran over her cheeks and dropped into her mouth and spotted the navy blue dress.

Ding, dong, ding, dong, went the schoolhouse bell. It meant that recess time was over.

"Come on, Tacy. We've *got* to go back."

Tacy cried harder than ever.

The lines of marching children vanished into the schoolhouse. A strange calm settled upon the empty yard. From an open window came the sound of children singing.

"We're supposed to be in there," Betsy said. She felt a queer frightened lump inside.

"You go back if you want to," said Tacy between sobs.

"I won't go back without you," said Betsy. She sat down miserably on Mrs. Chubbock's steps.

The door of the little store opened and Mrs. Chubbock came out. She was large and stout, with a small soft mustache. She leaned on a cane when she walked.

"What's this? What's this?" she asked. "Why aren't you in school?"

"We . . . we . . ." said Betsy. Her lip trembled.

"Aren't you supposed to be in school?"

"Yes, we are. But she . . . she's bashful."

"Runaways, eh?" said Mrs. Chubbock.

At the sound of the dread word, Betsy's eyes filled with tears. That was what they were exactly. Runaways. That was a terrible thing to be. How could she go home from school and tell her mamma? Would they ever be allowed to go to school again? Betsy too began to cry.

Once started, Betsy cried as hard as Tacy. Harder, perhaps. And when Tacy heard Betsy cry, she took a fresh start. They held each other tight and wailed.

"Now, now," said Mrs. Chubbock. She limped back

into her store. When she came out, she opened her two hands and each of them held a little chocolate man.

"Do you eat the head first or the legs first?" Mrs. Chubbock asked.

Betsy ate the head first and Tacy ate the legs first. They couldn't very well eat and cry together. So they were eating and not crying when they saw Miss Dalton hurrying across the schoolhouse yard. The sun was shining on her canary-colored hair. She looked pretty but very worried.

"Oh, there you are!" she cried gladly when she saw them. "You weren't supposed to go home, my dears. That was only recess."

The tears began to trickle again.

"I know," said Betsy. "But Tacy doesn't like school. She's bashful."

"And she won't go if I won't," said Tacy.

"No, I won't go if she won't," said Betsy. They lifted anxious faces, smeared with chocolate and tears.

Miss Dalton stooped down and put an arm around each of them. She smiled up at Mrs. Chubbock.

"Tacy," she said. "How would you like to sit with Betsy? Right in the same seat?"

So they went back to school. Tacy sat with Betsy, right in the same seat. They were crowded, but no more so than they were in the piano box. The little boy named Tom sat right behind them.

And after that Tacy liked school.

Betsy had liked it all the time.

6

The Milkman Story

EVERY MORNING Betsy called for Tacy, so that they could walk to school together.

Betsy came to Tacy's house a little early, usually, to be there when Tacy had her hair combed. There was a painful fascination in this business, for Tacy always cried.

Her ringlets were tangled after her night's sleep. When she washed for breakfast, they were merely tied back with a ribbon. Tacy's mother was busy getting breakfast for thirteen, and Tacy's curls took time. After breakfast the time for curls arrived. Tacy began to cry at sight of the comb.

Betsy's eyes grew round and she swayed back and forth as she watched. "But she cried harder than that, the first day of school, Mrs. Kelly."

"Then she must have cried pretty hard that day," Mrs. Kelly would answer. "Keep still, Tacy. I'm trying not to hurt."

Mrs. Kelly was stout and gentle. She was like a large, anxious dove. She was different from Betsy's mother who was slim and red-headed and gay. Betsy's mother knew how to scold as well as to laugh and sing. But Tacy's mother never scolded.

"If I tried to scold eleven I'd be scolding all the time," she explained to Betsy one day.

After the curls were brushed over Tacy's mother's finger, Betsy and Tacy started off to school. They walked to school together, and they walked home together. Back and forth together, every day.

At first it was autumn; there were red and yellow leaves for Betsy and Tacy to scuffle under foot. Then the leaves were brown, then they were blown away; that was in the gray time named November. Then came the exciting first snow, and this was followed by more snow and more. At last the drifts rising beside the sidewalk were higher than their heads.

Betsy and Tacy lay down in the drifts and spread out their arms to make angels. They rolled the snow into balls and had battles with Julia and Katie. They started a snowman in the vacant lot, and added to him day after day until . . . before a thaw came . . . he was as fat as Mrs. Chubbock.

The snow was fun while there was sun to glitter on it from a sky as bright and blue as Tacy's eyes. But after a time the weather grew cold; it was too cold for Betsy and Tacy to play in the snow any more. Their hands inside mittens ached, and their feet inside overshoes grew numb. The wind nipped their faces in their snugly tied hoods; their breath froze on the bright scarves knotted around their necks.

On days like that, as they walked home from school, Betsy told Tacy the milkman story.

It started one day when a milkman passed them on the corner by the chocolate-colored house. His wagon was running on runners; and it wasn't an ordinary wagon; it looked like a little house. The milkman sat covered with buffalo robes, and from deep in shadows came the glimmer of a fire. It might have come from the milkman's pipe, but Betsy and Tacy thought that it came from a little stove inside the milkman's wagon.

That gave Betsy the idea for a story.

The story went differently on different days, but one day it went like this:

Two little girls named Betsy and Tacy were walking home from school. It was very cold.

"I wish we could catch a ride," said Tacy.

And just at that moment a milkman came riding by. He was riding in a wagon which looked like a little house. He had a little stove inside. He said to Betsy and Tacy:

"Hello, little girls. Wouldn't you like a ride in this wagon? I'm through delivering milk, so you can have it for yourselves."

Betsy and Tacy said, "Thank you very much!" And the milkman jumped out, and they jumped in. And the milkman went away.

But before he went away he said, "You don't need to drive that horse. It's a pretty cold day for keeping hold of reins. Just wind the reins around the whip."

So Betsy and Tacy wound the reins around the whip, and they said to the horse, "Take us home, horse." The milkman's horse was a magic horse, but nobody knew it except the milkman and Betsy and Tacy.

The horse started off over the snow. The sleigh-bells jingled on his back, and the wagon ran so smoothly that it hardly joggled Betsy and Tacy. They were sitting beside the little stove in the very inside of the wagon. They were sitting on two little stools beside the stove.

In just a minute they were as warm as toast. It was cozy sitting there with the wagon sliding along. Only by and by Tacy said, "I'm hungry."

And Betsy said, "That's funny. Look what I see!" And she pointed over to a corner of the wagon, and there were two baskets. One was marked, "Betsy," and one was marked, "Tacy." They were covered with little red cloths.

Betsy and Tacy took off these cloths and spread them on their knees, and they looked into their baskets. Each one found a cup of cocoa there. It was hot. It was steaming. And it hadn't spilled a drop. That was because the milkman's wagon was magic like his horse.

And beside each cup of cocoa were doughnuts. They were hot too. They smelled like Mrs. Ray's doughnuts smell when she lifts them out of the lard on a fork. They smelled good. There were plenty of doughnuts for Betsy and plenty for Tacy.

"Isn't this fun?" Tacy said. "Riding along in the milkman's wagon and eating doughnuts?"

Just then the horse turned his head. "Those doughnuts smell good," he said.

"Oh, excuse me," said Betsy and Tacy. "We didn't know that horses ate doughnuts."

"Well, *I* do," said the horse. "Of course I'm a magic horse."

And Betsy and Tacy put three doughnuts on the whip and they held out the whip and the horse opened his mouth and the doughnuts dropped right in.

"Thank you," said the horse. "I'll take you home every day it's cold. I'll meet you where I met you today, on the corner by the chocolate-colored house."

In a minute he turned his head and said, "Of course it's a secret."

"Oh, yes," said Betsy and Tacy. "We understand that."

They had come so far now that they had come to Hill Street Hill. They were halfway up. They put their cups back in the baskets and covered the baskets with the red cloths, and they climbed out of the wagon.

"Thank you, horse," they said.

"You're welcome," said the horse.

They were almost up Hill Street Hill, and they weren't cold at all, hardly, on account of the ride they'd had.

Julia and Katie were just ahead.

"Hurry up!" they called. "Hurry up so you don't get frost bite."

"Frost bite!" said Betsy and Tacy, and they looked at each other and laughed.

"We're warm as toast," said Betsy, stamping her feet.

"We're hardly cold at all," said Tacy, swinging her arms.

Betsy said to Tacy, "Let's go ask your mamma if you can't bring your paper dolls and come over to my house to play."

"Yes, let's," said Tacy. "I hope we meet that milkman again tomorrow. Don't you, Betsy?"

"Those were good doughnuts," said Betsy. "Maybe my mamma will give us some more."

7
Playing Paper Dolls

QUITE OFTEN, after school, Betsy and Tacy went to Betsy's house and played paper dolls.

Betsy and Tacy liked paper dolls better than real dolls. They wanted real dolls too, of course. The most important thing to see on Christmas morning, poking out of a stocking or sitting under a tree, was a big china doll . . . with yellow curls and a blue silk dress and bonnet, or with black curls and a pink silk dress and bonnet . . . it didn't matter which. But after Christmas they put those dolls away and played with their paper dolls.

They cut the paper dolls from fashion magazines. They could hardly wait for their mothers' magazines to grow old. Mrs. Benson didn't have any children, so she saved her fashion magazines for Betsy and Tacy. And when Miss Meade, the sewing woman, came to Betsy's house, she could be depended upon to leave a magazine or two behind.

The chief trouble Betsy and Tacy had was in finding pictures of men and boys. There had to be father dolls and brother dolls, of course. The tailor shops had men's fashion sheets. But those fashion sheets were hard to get. Tacy's brother George worked next door to a tailor shop. He told Mr. Baumgarten, the tailor, that his little sister Tacy liked those fashion sheets. After that Mr. Baumgarten saved all his fashion sheets for Tacy, and Tacy divided them with Betsy.

The dolls were not only cut from magazines; they lived in magazines. Betsy and Tacy each had a doll family living in a magazine. The servant dolls were kept in a pile between the first two pages; a few pages on was the pile of father dolls; then came the mother dolls, and then the sixteen-year-olds, the ten-year-olds, the eight-year-olds, the five-year-olds, and the babies.

Those were the dolls that Betsy and Tacy played with after school.

Betsy and Tacy stopped in at Tacy's house to get her magazine and eat a cookie. Then they went on to Betsy's house, and when Betsy had kissed her mother and both of them had hung their wraps in the little closet off the back parlor, Betsy brought out the magazine in which her doll family lived.

"Shall we play here beside the stove, Mamma?" she asked.

"Yes, that would be a good place to play," said Mrs. Ray; and it was.

The fire glowed red through the isinglass windows of the big hard coal heater. It shone on the wild horses' heads which ran in a procession around the shining nickel trim. Up on the warming ledge the tea kettle was singing. Underneath the stove, on the square metal plate which protected the green flowered carpet, Lady Jane Grey, the cat, was singing too.

She opened one sleepy eye but she kept on purring as Betsy and Tacy opened their magazines.

"What shall we name the five-year-old today?" Tacy asked Betsy.

The five-year-olds were the most important members of the large doll families. Everything pleasant happened to them. They had all the adventures.

The eight-year-olds lived very dull lives; and they were always given very plain names. They were Jane and Martha, usually, or Hannah and Jemima. Sometimes Betsy and Tacy forgot and called them Julia and Katie. But the five-year-olds had beautiful names. They were Lucille and Evelyn, or Madeline and Millicent.

"We'll be Madeline and Millicent today," Betsy decided.

They played that it was morning. The servant dolls got up first. The servant dolls wore caps with long streamers and dainty ruffled aprons. They didn't look at all like the hired girls of Hill Street. But like hired girls they got up bright and early.

The fathers and mothers got up next. Then came the children beginning with the oldest. The five-year-olds came dancing down to breakfast in the fingers of Betsy and Tacy.

"What are you planning to do today, Madeline?" Betsy's father doll asked his five-year-old.

"I'm going to play with Millicent, Papá." (Madeline and Millicent pronounced papa, papá.)

"And I'm going to play with Jemima," said Betsy's eight-year-old who was named Hannah today.

"No, Hannah!" said her father. "You must stay at home and wash the dishes. But Madeline may go. Wouldn't you like to take the carriage, Madeline? You and Millicent could go for a nice ride. Here is a dollar in case you want some candy."

"Oh, thank you, Papá," said Madeline. She gave him an airy kiss.

Meanwhile Tacy's dolls were talking in much the same way. Both father dolls were sent quickly down to work; the mothers went shopping; the babies were taken out in their carriages by the pretty servant dolls; and the older children were shut in the magazines. Then Betsy and Tacy each took her five-year-old in hand, and the fun of the game began.

First they went to the candy store under the patent rocker. Madeline's dollar bought an enormous quantity of gum drops and candy corn. Next they sat down in their carriage which was made of a shoebox. There were two strings attached, and Betsy and Tacy were the horses. Madeline and Millicent took a beautiful ride.

They climbed the back parlor sofa; that was a mountain.

"Let's have a picnic," said Madeline. So they did. They picnicked on top of a pillow which had the head of a girl embroidered on it.

They swished through the dangling bamboo

curtains which separated the back parlor from the front parlor. And in the front parlor they left their carriage again. They climbed the piano stool; that was a merry-go-round, and of course they had a ride.

After calling on Mrs. Vanderbilt, who lived behind the starched lace curtains at the front parlor window, and Mrs. Astor, who lived under an easel which was draped in purple silk, they slipped by way of the dining room into the back parlor again.

And here they met with their greatest adventure!

The Betsy horse began to rear and snort.

"What's the matter?" asked the Tacy horse.

"A tiger! A tiger!" cried the Betsy horse. She jumped and kicked.

The Tacy horse began to jump and kick too, looking about her for the tiger. Lady Jane Grey was awake and washing her face.

"She's getting ready to

eat us!" cried the Betsy horse, leaping.

"Help!" cried the Tacy horse, leaping too.

They leaped so high that they overturned the carriage. Out went Madeline and Millicent on the highway of the green flowered carpet.

"We're running away!" shouted the Betsy horse.

"Whoa! Whoa!" shouted the Tacy horse.

They ran through the rattling bamboo curtains into the front parlor. There they stopped being horses and raced back, out of breath, to be Madeline and Millicent again.

Lady Jane Grey loved to play with paper. She entered obligingly into the game.

"He's biting me!" shrieked Madeline.

"He's scratching me!" shrieked Millicent.

The tiger growled and pounced.

Madeline and Millicent were rescued just in time. The father dolls rushed up and seized them and jumped into the coal scuttle. Lady Jane Grey jumped in too and jumped out looking black instead of gray, and Betsy and Tacy scrambled in the coal scuttle trying to fish out the father dolls before they got too black. There were never enough father dolls, in spite of Mr. Baumgarten.

Julia and Katie came in just then from skating. The opening door brought in a rush of winter cold and dark.

"Well, for goodness' sake!" they cried. *"For goodness' sake!"* They cried it so loud that Betsy's mother came in from the kitchen, where she was getting supper.

"Betsy!" she cried. "Come straight out here and wash! And use soap and a wash cloth and warm water from the kettle! You too, Tacy."

"Yes, ma'am," said Betsy and Tacy.

When they had washed they put their paper dolls back into the magazines. And Katie helped Tacy into her outside wraps and took her by the hand, and they started home.

Right at the door, Tacy turned around to smile at Betsy. "Whoa!" she said, instead of "Good-by!"

"Giddap!" said Betsy, instead of "Come again!"

"Whoa!" "Giddap!" "Whoa!" "Giddap!" they said over and over.

"Whatever are you two talking about?" said Julia and Katie crossly, which was just what Betsy and Tacy had hoped they would say.

8

Easter Eggs

JULIA AND Katie were nice sometimes. They were nice when it came time to color Easter eggs. That happened a few days before Easter. It seemed to be still winter. There was lots of snow outside, and coal still went rattling into the back parlor stove, but Betsy and Tacy knew that spring was near. All of a sudden they didn't care a bit about sliding down hill on their sleds. All they could think or talk about was coloring Easter eggs.

They colored the eggs in Betsy's kitchen. Tacy's little sister Beatrice was sick. She was Bee, the baby, and she was very sick. Mrs. Ray kept Katie and Tacy over at her house all she could.

Julia and Katie put on big aprons and acted important, but not too important. They let Betsy and Tacy help, coloring the eggs.

First they collected all the cups they could find which had handles missing and cracks along the sides. Then they dissolved the dye in warm water from the kettle, each color in a different cup. The eggs were placed in the cups for a while, and when they were taken out they were red or purple or orange. The colors were so bright . . . it was thrilling to look at them.

On Easter morning everyone ate as many eggs as he could. At Betsy's house, they did.

"I ate three," said Betsy, when Tacy came running over to ask. "And my papa ate five."

"I ate three, too," said Tacy. "And last year my brother George ate ten. But this year nobody paid much attention to eggs at our house, except Katie and Paul and me."

That was because Baby Bee was sick.

They went to church, though, from Tacy's house.

Everyone in the family went, except Tacy's mother who stayed home with Bee. And Tacy had a new hat (navy blue, because she had red hair). It was straw and showed her ears and had stiff gay flowers on the top.

Betsy had a new hat which looked much the same, and she went to church too with her father and mother and Julia. Her mother sang in the choir, and the church smelled of lilies. Betsy liked Easter.

She liked it especially after church, for Katie and Tacy came to dinner. They had chicken, and everyone was very well behaved. After dinner they sat by the back parlor stove and played with their colored eggs.

Katie and Tacy were to stay until they were called for. By and by it grew dark. Mrs. Ray said, wouldn't it be fun if they could stay all night? Katie could sleep with Julia, and Tacy with Betsy. But after supper Mr. Kelly came over.

"Thank you very much," he said. "But Mrs. Kelly wants the children home."

Tacy put her colored eggs into the pocket of her coat. She went home and the next day she didn't come over. She didn't come over the next day, nor the next, for Baby Bee died. Betsy's father and mother went to the funeral.

Betsy was very lonesome for Tacy. The next

morning she went out early before anyone was up. She often went out early in the summer time; Tacy did too. But it was strange going out early at this time of year.

Betsy dressed in all her warm clothes, just as she knew she should. She dressed without waking Julia, and she stole down the stairs without waking her father and mother, and she got her coat and hood and overshoes and mittens out of the back parlor closet and put them on softly and went softly out of the side kitchen door.

The lilac bush stood by that door. It didn't seem to be awake. The snow which had melted yesterday had frozen in the night, and it hadn't come unfrozen yet. Everything in Hill Street seemed to be waiting for the sun. The trees and houses waited in a dim gray light. Behind the white house which stood on the Big Hill, the sky was colored pink.

Betsy walked over to Tacy's house and looked at the upstairs windows.

Tacy must have known that Betsy would come over. After a while she came out of the house. She too had gotten up without waking a soul. She had put on everything warm, the way she knew her mamma would want her to—her coat and hood and overshoes and mittens. She even had her scarf tied around her neck.

She and Betsy looked at each other, and then they started walking.

"What shall we do?" asked Tacy.

"Let's climb a tree," said Betsy.

It wasn't the time of year for climbing trees, but Betsy and Tacy were great tree climbers. So they climbed a tree.

They didn't climb Betsy's backyard maple which was their favorite tree to climb. They went up the Big Hill until they found a tree with branches low enough to reach, and they climbed that and sat there.

Somewhere a bird was singing a little up and down song. They couldn't see him but they could hear him. His busy up and down song was the only sound in the world. Hill Street was still sleeping, but the color in the sky was spreading. Gold sticks in the shape of a fan were sticking up over the hill.

After a while Tacy said, "It smelled like Easter in the church. Bee looked awful pretty. She had candles all around her."

"Did she?" asked Betsy.

"But my mamma felt awful bad," said Tacy.

Betsy said nothing.

"Of course," said Tacy, "you know that Bee has only gone to Heaven."

"Oh, of course," said Betsy.

But Tacy's lip was shaking. That made Betsy feel queer. So she said quickly, "Heaven's awful nice."

"Is it?" asked Tacy, looking toward her. Her eyes were big and full of trouble.

"Yes," said Betsy. "It's like that sunrise. In fact," she added, "that's it. We can't see it during the day, but early in the morning they let us have a peek."

"It's pretty," said Tacy, staring.

"Those gold sticks you see, those are candles," said Betsy. "There's a gold-colored light all the time. And there are harps to play on; they're something like pianos. But you don't need to take any lessons. You just know how to play. Bee's having a good time up there," said Betsy, looking up into the sky.

Tacy looked too. "Can she see us?"

"Of course she can see us. She's looking down right now. And I'll tell you what tickles Bee. She knows all about Heaven, and we don't. She's younger than we are, but she knows something we don't know. Isn't that funny? She's just a baby, and she knows more than we do."

"And more than Julia and Katie do," said Tacy.

"Even more than our fathers and mothers do," said Betsy. "It's funny when you come to think of it."

"She's a long way from home though," said Tacy.

"But she gets all the news," said Betsy. "Do you

know how she gets it? Why, from the birds. They fly up there and tell her how you are and what you're all doing down at your house."

"Do they?" asked Tacy.

And just at that moment, the little up and down song stopped, and there flew past them, going right up the hill, a robin red breast. He was the first robin they had seen that spring, and he was as red as a red Easter egg. He flew up the hill fast, as though he knew where he was going.

"He's going to see Bee, of course," Betsy said. "He'll be back in a minute."

Tacy put her hand in her pocket, and it touched the colored Easter eggs she had brought from Betsy's house.

"Betsy," she said, "do you suppose he'd take one of these Easter eggs to Bee?"

"Of course he would," said Betsy. "The only trouble is how to give it to him."

She looked about her. She looked up, and high up in the tree was a nest. It was a big ragged nest. It looked as though it had been there all winter. But it was a nest; it was a bird's house.

"Give me the egg," she said. "Which one are you sending?"

"The purple one," said Tacy. "It's the prettiest."

"I'll put it in that nest," said Betsy. "The robin

can take it up in his mouth."

So Betsy took the purple egg, and she put it in the pocket of her coat. And she climbed up the tree, higher than she had ever gone before. She didn't look down; she looked up instead. She held on tight with her arms to the rough trunk of the tree, and she felt for the branches with her feet.

She climbed to the very top of the tree, and put the purple egg in the nest.

"There!" she said when she came back to Tacy. "Bee will like that egg."

They scrambled down the tree and skipped down the hill. The sunrise was almost finished. A pale surprised light was spreading over Hill Street. Smoke was coming out of kitchen chimneys here and there.

"Dyeing those Easter eggs was fun," said Tacy.

"Yes," said Betsy, "and I saved the dye. Mamma was going to throw it out, but I teased her, and she let me have it."

"What will we do with it?" asked Tacy.

"I don't know exactly. But something. You'll see."

So they skipped down the Big Hill to breakfast. They were hungry, too. And for once no one was calling "Betsy" and "Tacy." No one was awake to call.

9
The Sand Store

THAT SPRING Betsy's father built a room on their house. He said, "What if our family should grow bigger? There's a bedroom for mother and me, and one for Julia and Betsy. But what about Robert Ray Junior, when he comes along?"

So he hired a mason and a carpenter, and they built another bedroom. It was downstairs, tucked into the corner between the back parlor and the kitchen. It was going to belong to Betsy's father and mother after all. Robert Junior could have one of the upstairs bedrooms, Betsy's father said.

Betsy and Tacy thought it was exciting to have a room built on. They played see-saw on the clean, good-smelling planks. They made curls for their dolls out of the fresh yellow shavings. They dug in the sandpile which the mason had left.

That sand was what started the sand store.

Betsy and Tacy had played store lots of times. The piano box had been first one kind of store and then another, the summer before. It had been a millinery store, full of hats made from maple leaves, and it had been a lemonade store, where they sold lemonade. Now it became a sand store, on account of the fresh new sand.

It happened on the first, good, play-out Saturday in spring. The sun was warm over the earth. Robins and bluebirds and orioles flew in and out of the newly leaved maples, singing as they went. The air smelled sweet from the blooming plum trees in Betsy's father's orchard and the plumy purple lilacs by the side kitchen door. Julia and Katie had gone up on the hill to pick flowers. But Betsy and Tacy had stayed to play in the sand.

The sand was so white and pretty that Betsy got an idea.

"Let's put it in bottles and sell it," she said.

"Where will we get the bottles?" asked Tacy.

"Oh, we'll ask our mammas and Mrs. Benson," said Betsy.

So she and Tacy ran to get the bottles.

Betsy's mother gave them an olive bottle and a pickle bottle and a catsup bottle. And Tacy's mother gave them a pickle bottle and a catsup bottle and a big fat jar. And Mrs. Benson gave them a catsup bottle and a pickle bottle and a perfume bottle with a blue colored stopper. Betsy and Tacy washed all the bottles and took them to the sand pile.

"Now we'll fill them," said Betsy, and they each began on a pickle bottle, putting the sand in with spoons.

Tacy held her bottle up to the sun and looked at it. "I wish that sand was colored like our Easter eggs," she said.

Then Betsy jumped up, and began to jump up and down.

"Tacy!" she cried. "I saved those Easter egg dyes. They're put away in bottles in our piano box."

And sure enough, they were! They were hidden in a corner under a pile of yellow shaving curls, and some Sunday School cards and a box where a turtle had lived. There was green dye and yellow and purple and red and blue.

Betsy and Tacy ran into their houses and got cups (the cups with handles missing and cracks along the sides). They emptied the dye into the cups and put sand into the dye and they left it in the dye until it was colored. Then they spread it out on one of the new planks, each color in a different heap.

While it dried they sang a song which Betsy made up. It went like this:

> "Oh, the Easter egg dyes,
> The Easter egg dyes,
> We could make this sand
> Into Easter egg pies.
> But we're going to fill beautiful
> Bottles instead
> With Easter egg yellow
> And Easter egg red."

At dinner time Julia and Katie came down from the hill with their hands full of violets and hepaticas, blood roots and Dutchmen's Breeches. They stopped and stared when they saw the colored sand.

"Well, for goodness' sake!" they said. And then they said, "We'll help you fill those bottles after dinner."

Julia and Katie were nice sometimes. Besides it was fun, filling the bottles.

The vanilla bottle and the catsup bottles were

filled with sand of just one color. That was because they were hard to fill; their necks were small. The other bottles had sand in layers . . . purple with yellow, green with red, red with blue.

The jar that Tacy's mother had given them was the prettiest of all. Into that one they had put sand of every color. The mouth of the jar was wide, so that the stripes could be made smooth and even. It made Betsy throb inside to see the shining colors through the glass.

When they had finished, Julia jumped up. "Now I've got to practice my music lesson," she said.

"I've got to take care of Paul," Katie said.

Betsy and Tacy didn't care.

In front of the piano box they put two chunks of wood, the kind that Betsy's mother burned in the kitchen stove. Across those chunks they laid one of the planks from the room Betsy's father had built. They got a cigar box to hold their money, and Tacy sat behind the counter, and Betsy called, "Sand for sale! Sand for sale!" She called it as loud as she could.

At last the children began to come, all the children of Hill Street.

They bought bottles of sand and they paid for them with pins. The bottom of the cigar box was glittery with pins. But Betsy and Tacy wouldn't sell their two best bottles for pins. They wouldn't sell the perfume bottle with the blue colored stopper nor the big fat jar.

"We'll sell them to Mrs. Benson," they said.

So when all the rest of the bottles were gone, they went to Mrs. Benson's house.

She was busy getting supper, but she stopped to admire the bottles.

"What beautiful bottles of sand!" she said. "How much do you ask for them?"

"We don't know," said Betsy and Tacy.

"Would five cents apiece be enough?"

"Five cents apiece!" said Betsy and Tacy. They were astounded.

Mrs. Benson gave them each a nickel, and put the big fat jar on her piano and the perfume bottle on her parlor table.

"Don't they look beautiful!" she said.

Betsy and Tacy thought they did.

Halfway up the hill, Betsy said, "Five cents is a terrible lot of money."

"I know it," Tacy said.

"I'm not sure," said Betsy. "But I *think* that five and five make nine."

"I'm sure they do," said Tacy. "I've heard Katie talking about it."

"It's a lot of money to keep around and not spend," said Betsy.

After a moment Tacy said, "We could go to Mrs. Chubbock's."

"No," said Betsy. "You only need pennies to buy candy. These are *nickels*. We can buy something more important than candy."

She thought and she thought.

"Do you know what I think we'd better buy?" she asked, after she had thought.

"What?" asked Tacy.

"That chocolate-colored house."

"The one we pass when we go to school?" asked Tacy.

"With the tower," said Betsy. "And the pane of colored glass over the door."

"What would we do with it when we got it?" asked Tacy.

"Why, live in it. We'd sleep in the room with the tower."

"We could look through that colored glass whenever we pleased," Tacy said.

So they decided to go and buy the chocolate-colored house.

At the vacant lot they met one of Tacy's brothers. It was George, the one who asked the tailor for fashion sheets for Tacy.

"Aren't you two a long way from home?" he asked.

"We go to school this way every day," Tacy said.

"But this isn't school time. This is supper time," said George. As he spoke the whistle blew for six o'clock.

"Well, it's like this," said Betsy. "Tacy and I earned a lot of money today."

"So you're going to Mrs. Chubbock's."

"No," said Tacy. "We're going to buy a house."

"A house! What house?"

"That house," said Betsy and Tacy, and they pointed through the trees on the vacant lot to the corner of the street beyond. You could see, quite plainly, the tower of the chocolate-colored house.

"How much money have you got?" asked George.

"Nine cents," said Tacy.

"We *think* it's nine cents," said Betsy. They opened their hands and showed him the two nickels.

George pulled his mouth down hard, as though he were thinking.

"It's lots of money, all right," he said. "It isn't quite enough, though, to buy that house. I wouldn't buy it today if I were you. What are we having for supper, Tacy?"

"I don't know," said Tacy. She hung her head in disappointment. Betsy swallowed hard.

"Maybe it's near enough summer," said George,

"so that you two could take your plates up on the hill. Do you remember how you used to do that?"

"Oh, yes!" cried Tacy.

"It was fun," cried Betsy.

They had almost forgotten how they used to eat on the hill.

They looked up Hill Street, and the hill seemed to have been painted with a light green brush. Their little bench was waiting in the rosy sunset light.

"I'll go ask my mamma," said Betsy.

"I'll go ask my mamma, too," said Tacy.

They both started to run.

"And put those nickels in the bank," George called. "Save them! Do you hear?"

But Betsy and Tacy were running too fast to hear.

10

Calling on Mrs. Benson

WHEN SUMMER TIME came Betsy and Tacy didn't need to bother with school any more. They could play all day long. They did play all day long, and they never once ran out of things to do.

"The days aren't long enough for those two," Betsy's mother used to say to Betsy's father.

This was true; although it was strange, for a day was very long.

A day filled all the hours which it took the sun to wheel from behind the white house on the Big Hill, across the vast blue spaces of the sky, to the trees down behind Tacy's barn. By the time evening came and Betsy and Tacy were playing games with the other Hill Street children (not made-up games, but real games, like Pom Pom Pullaway and Run, Sheep, Run), they could hardly remember the cool morning hours when they had had the world to themselves. But in all the long golden time in between, they never ran out of games to play.

One of their favorite games was dressing up. They loved to dress up in grown-up clothes and go calling.

One day Betsy's mother let her dress up in her old tan lace dress. It was a beautiful dress with a big pink rose in the front. Betsy poked an old table cloth underneath her skirts behind to make a bustle like her mother's. And she wore an old hat of her mother's, a round hat with a veil.

Tacy wore a striped blue and green silk dress of her grown-up sister Mary's. Her curls were pinned high, and she wore a big hat covered with flowers. And Mary let her carry her parasol, which was pink with ruffles all around it.

When Tacy was given the parasol, she and Betsy raced back to Betsy's house.

"Mamma," Betsy cried, "Tacy has a parasol. May I carry your parasol?"

"No," said Betsy's mother. "But you may carry my cardcase." She got it out of the bureau drawer. One side was filled with cards which said "Mrs. Robert Ray." A little lace-edged handkerchief, smelling of violet perfume, peeked out of the other side. Betsy's mother carried this case when she went calling. She left a card at every house.

Betsy took the cardcase and Tacy opened the parasol, and they started down Hill Street.

"We'll call on Mrs. Benson," Betsy said.

So they called on Mrs. Benson, and she was very glad to see them.

"Come right in," she said. "How are you, Mrs. Ray? How do you do, Mrs. Kelly?"

She pretended that they were their mothers, instead of Betsy and Tacy. Of course that was the right thing to do.

"Sit right down," she said, and they sat down on the sofa. "It's lovely weather we're having."

"Yes, isn't it?" said Betsy in a very grown-up tone. Tacy didn't talk much; she was bashful.

"I hear you bought some sand, Mrs. Benson," said Betsy in the grown-up tone.

"Yes, I did. Would you like to see it?" asked Mrs. Benson, and she went to her desk and brought out the two bottles full of sand which Betsy and Tacy had colored, the perfume bottle with the blue colored stopper and the big fat jar.

"Mercy, what beautiful sand!" said Betsy.

"Isn't it!" cried Mrs. Benson. "I bought it from two little girls named Betsy and Tacy."

Tacy looked up then, her blue eyes dancing into Mrs. Benson's. "I know those little girls," she said.

"I thought maybe you did," said Mrs. Benson.

After a minute Mrs. Benson asked, "Wouldn't

you like some tea?"

"Tea?" asked Betsy, so surprised that she forgot to talk like her mother.

"Afternoon tea," explained Mrs. Benson. "What ladies drink when they go calling."

"Oh, of course," said Betsy. "I'd love some. Wouldn't you, Tacy?"

So Mrs. Benson gave them some tea . . . cambric tea, she called it, and it was delicious. They had cookies with their tea, and Betsy and Tacy nibbled them daintily. But they ate them to the very last crumb.

When the cookies were gone, Betsy said, "Well,

I'm afraid we'll have to be going. Good-by, Mrs. Benson."

"Good-by, Mrs. Ray," Mrs. Benson said.

"Good-by, Mrs. Benson," said Tacy, not bashful any more.

"Good-by, Mrs. Kelly," said Mrs. Benson. "May I help you open your parasol?"

Then Betsy remembered the cardcase.

"And I must leave you a card," she said. "Here's a card for me and one for Tacy."

Betsy and Tacy went on, down Hill Street Hill.

"Who shall we call on next?" asked Tacy.

"I know," said Betsy. "We'll call at the chocolate-colored house."

So they went on down Hill Street Hill to the corner and through the vacant lot. It was farther than they had ever gone before in grown-up clothes. They held their long skirts high so that the weeds and bushes would not tear them, and they came to the chocolate-colored house.

"Tacy," said Betsy, "I never yet saw anybody around this chocolate-colored house."

"Neither did I," said Tacy.

They looked at it a moment before they climbed to the door.

It sat like a big plump chocolate drop on the big square corner lot. There weren't many trees around it; just a green lawn with flower beds on either side of the white cement walk which led to the porch steps.

Betsy and Tacy walked up that walk and climbed the porch steps.

They rang the bell and waited.

While they were waiting they looked around. The tower jutted right out on the porch. It had windows in it, but all the shades were pulled down. The pane of colored glass over the front door shone

ruby red in the sunlight.

No one answered their ring, and Betsy and Tacy rang the bell again. They rang it again and again.

At last the lady next door came out of her house. She looked busy and cross.

"What are you doing on that porch, little girls?" she asked in a sharp voice.

"We're ringing the bell," said Betsy. "We've come to call."

"Tell her about the cardcase," whispered Tacy.

But before Betsy could speak again, the lady said, "Well, the people who live there aren't home. They've gone to Milwaukee."

She went back into her house and shut the door.

"Milwaukee," said Betsy.

"Milwaukee," said Tacy.

They liked the sound of the word.

"I wish I could go to Milwaukee," said Betsy.

"What's it like?" asked Tacy.

"Oh, it's lovely," said Betsy. "Milwaukee. Milwaukee." She said the name over and over.

"While we walk home," she said to Tacy, "I'll make up a poem about it." Betsy liked to make up poems.

"First we must leave a card, though," said Tacy.

"Of course," said Betsy.

They opened the cardcase and took out a card

and put it in the mailbox. Mrs. Robert Ray, it said on the card. They took out another and left that one too. The second one was from Tacy.

While they walked home, Betsy made up the poem about Milwaukee. It went like this:

"There's a place named Milwaukee, Milwaukee,
Milwaukee, Milwauk, MilwaukEE,
There's a place named Milwaukee, Milwaukee,
A beautiful place to be;
I wish I could go to Milwaukee,
With Tacy ahold of my hand,
I wish I could go to Milwaukee,
It sounds like the Beulah Land."

"That's a nice poem," said Tacy. "I like the part about me."

So they sang it together, making up a tune. They sang it all the way through the vacant lot. And just at the edge of the vacant lot they saw Betsy's father who was driving home for supper. He was driving Old Mag and had just slowed down for Hill Street Hill.

"Stop!" "Wait!" "Give us a ride!" cried Betsy and Tacy. They picked up their long skirts and began to run.

"Why, how do you do, Mrs. Vanderbilt?" said

Betsy's father. "And how do you do, Mrs. Astor?"

He stopped Old Mag and cramped the wheel of the buggy, and Betsy and Tacy climbed in.

Betsy took the reins and Tacy held the whip. Julia and Katie were watching from the steps of the Ray house.

"Giddap!" said Betsy.

"Whoa!" said Tacy.

They drove in triumph around the little road which led to Old Mag's barn.

11

The Buggy Shed

ETSY AND Tacy liked to ride home with
Betsy's father, or Tacy's. Along about sunset they would walk to the foot of Hill
Street Hill and wait. Sometimes they rode up the
hill with Mr. Ray and sometimes with Mr. Kelly.
Always they rode around to the barn and helped to
feed and water the horse, and saw straw put down

for his bed and the buggy rolled into the buggy shed.

During the day they liked to play in Betsy's buggy shed. It was dark and smelled of hay and oats from the barn which stood right beside it. When Old Mag was in the barn they could hear her chewing oats and stamping flies, but she wasn't often there. She was gone to the store and so was the buggy. Only the surrey was left in the buggy shed for Betsy and Tacy to play with.

The surrey had two seats and a canopy edged with fringe. There was a pocket in one corner for the whip, and a dust robe to spread on their laps. It was used mostly on Sundays when the family went to church or took a picnic to the river, and on summer evenings when they sometimes went riding while their bedrooms cooled off after the heat of the day.

"Shall we sit in the front seat or the back seat?" asked Tacy now, as she and Betsy climbed in.

"The front seat," said Betsy. For children usually sat in the back seat. So Betsy and Tacy sat in the front seat, and Betsy picked up the whip. Tacy tucked the robe around them, although it was a very warm day.

"Giddap!" said Betsy, cracking the whip.

"Don't go too fast," said Tacy.

"I won't," said Betsy. "I think too much of my horse." That was what her father said, so she knew it was the proper thing to say.

Through the open door of the buggy shed, they could see the Big Hill. It was pleasantly green with an arc of blue above it.

"See things fly past!" said Betsy. "Streets and houses and things."

"Where are we going?" asked Tacy.

"To Milwaukee," said Betsy.

"Goodie!" said Tacy. "That's the place I want most of all to see."

"Well, you're going there now," said Betsy, and she cracked the whip again. "Tuck up good," she said.

"Did we bring a lunch?" asked Tacy.

"Yes," said Betsy. "It's under the seat. There are chicken sandwiches and hard-boiled eggs and potato salad and watermelon and chocolate cake and sweet pickles and sugar cookies and ice cream."

"It ought to be plenty," Tacy said.

They went down Hill Street to Broad Street where the churches and the library and the big houses were; and they turned from Broad Street to Front Street where the stores were. They went past the office where Tacy's father sold sewing machines and past the store where Betsy's father sold shoes.

But they didn't stop.

"We haven't time," said Betsy.

They went on down Front Street to the Big Mill at the end. That Big Mill blew the whistle for six o'clock in the morning and twelve o'clock noon and six o'clock at night. It wasn't blowing any whistles now. Betsy and Tacy rode past it. They rode up Front Street Hill and out of the town of Deep Valley. They were out in the country now.

"I think it's time for our lunch," Tacy said.

"Yes, it is," said Betsy. "We'll stop here beside this lake."

So they stopped beside a lake, and they let Old Mag's check rein down so that she could drink. And Betsy and Tacy sat down in the shade and opened their picnic basket.

"I just love chicken sandwiches," said Betsy.

"This ice cream is good," said Tacy. "It hasn't melted a bit."

"We must be careful not to squirt this watermelon," Betsy said.

"Yes," said Tacy. "We forgot to bring any napkins."

When they had finished eating they climbed back into the surrey and they rode and rode and rode.

"I see Milwaukee," Betsy said after a while.

"Do you?" asked Tacy. "Where?"

"See those towers a way, way off?" Betsy said. And when they had come closer, she said, "It looks like the cities on my Sunday School cards, with that wall and all those towers."

"That's right," said Tacy. "I see palm trees."

"The people will wear red and blue night gowns, like they do on the Sunday School cards, most likely," Betsy said.

"Maybe there will be camels," said Tacy.

"Of course there will be camels. I think I see a camel's head now, sticking around. . . ."

There was a head sticking around the side of the buggy shed door. But it didn't belong to a camel. It belonged to the little boy named Tom.

"Hello," he called out doubtfully.

"What are you doing here?" Betsy asked.

"My mother brought me. She came on an errand."

"Oh! Well, you can play with us if you want to."

"What are you playing?"

"We're going on a trip in this surrey."

"Where to?" he asked, coming in.

Betsy hesitated, and Tacy didn't speak either. They liked Tom; but boys were boys; they didn't always understand. And Milwaukee was no ordinary city. Milwaukee was their secret. They had a song about it.

"Just going on a trip," said Betsy. "Is there any-where you'd like to go?"

"Sure," said Tom. "I'd like to go to St. Paul. I went there once. Stayed at a hotel. And a man gave me a nickel. We went to St. Paul on a train though. Do you think that horse could make it?" he stared at the empty shafts.

"This is a fine horse," said Betsy. "And you may drive because you're company."

So she and Tacy didn't get to Milwaukee that day, after all. But they had a good time in St. Paul. They stayed in St. Paul until Julia and Katie came to tell them that there were lemonade and cookies for the children under the butternut tree.

12

Margaret

THAT SUMMER Julia and Betsy went for a visit to Uncle Edward's farm. They had a good time too. They saw the cows milked and they helped to gather eggs and they played with chicks and ducklings and they rode on the big farm wagons. But at last the time came to go home, and Betsy was glad. She wanted to tell Tacy all about it.

Betsy's father didn't come to get them. Uncle Edward drove them home. They drove into town and up Hill Street and up to the very end of Hill Street. Betsy was looking everywhere for Tacy; she wanted to tell her all about the farm.

But before she could find Tacy she saw her father. He was standing on the porch waving to them.

"Hurry!" he called. "I've got a surprise." And Uncle Edward began to laugh, and stopped the horse. And Julia and Betsy scrambled over the wheel and out of the buggy and ran up the steps of the little yellow cottage, to the porch where their father was waiting.

He was smiling all over his face, and he hugged them and kissed them and said, "Guess what's waiting for you inside the house."

Betsy thought and thought. And she knew they had a cat, so she was going to say, "A dog!" But Julia cried out, "Robert Ray Junior!"

Her father laughed out loud at that, and he gave her a squeeze. "Guess again," he said. And Julia said, "A little sister!" And Betsy's father said, "That's right. A little sister! And we can't very well call a girl Robert, so you and Betsy have to find a name for her. You can name her all by yourselves."

Betsy's father led the way into the house. For some reason he went on tiptoe. And he led the way

into the parlor and into the back parlor and into the
new downstairs bedroom, and there was Betsy's
mother lying in bed. And resting on her arm was a
little red-faced baby. A woman wearing a white
apron stood beside the bed.

"Julia! Betsy!" cried their mother. "Come here
and kiss me, and see your baby sister."

Julia and Betsy tiptoed toward the bed.

The room smelled of medicine, and the woman
with the white apron was strange, and Betsy felt
strange, too. And she didn't at all like the looks of
her baby sister! But her mother was gazing at them
with such shining eyes . . . Betsy couldn't bear to
hurt her feelings. So she didn't say a word.

Julia actually liked the baby. You could tell that she did. She "Oh-ed" and she "Ah-ed" and she said, "Oh, let me hold her. *May* I hold her, Papa?" And she lifted up one of the tiny hands and cried, "Isn't she darling?"

Betsy was disgusted with Julia. Julia never did have much sense, she thought to herself. When nobody was looking she slipped into the kitchen and out the back kitchen door.

She had thought that the first thing she would do when she got home would be to run over to Tacy's, but she didn't want to go to Tacy's now. She wanted to get away where nobody could see her, and for a very special reason. She went out past the back-yard maple and through the garden and the little orchard and past the buggy shed and into the barn. Old Mag was there munching hay. And Betsy went into a corner of the barn and sat down and began to cry.

She didn't know why she was crying except that everything was so queer. Her mamma in bed, a strange woman around, the room smelling of medicine and that *unnecessary* baby.

"It's a perfectly *unnecessary* baby," Betsy said aloud. "*I'm* the baby." And the more she thought that, the harder she cried, and the farther she scrunched away into a corner of the barn.

Bye and bye Tacy came in. Tacy hadn't seen Betsy go into the barn. She just seemed to know that Betsy was in that barn, as Betsy had known that Tacy would come outdoors early the morning after Baby Bee's funeral. Tacy came in, and she came straight over to the corner where Betsy was sitting, and she sat down beside her and put her arm around her. She held Betsy tight. Betsy went "sniff, sniff," "sniff, sniff," every two sniffs farther apart, until at last she wasn't crying any more. She was just sitting still inside Tacy's arm.

Then Tacy said, "Most everybody has babies, you know."

"Do they?" asked Betsy.

"Yes. Look at our house," said Tacy. "First I was the baby, and then Paul came. And then Paul was the baby, and then Bee came. And then Bee died so now Paul's the baby again. But I expect there'll be another baby most any time.

"You can't keep on being the baby forever," Tacy said, finishing up.

Somehow that made Betsy feel better, to know that Tacy used to be the baby and now wasn't the baby any more. Tacy got along all right. And if this was something that happened to everybody, having a new baby come to the house now and then, why it just had to happen to her.

"Our baby's funny looking," she said in a low voice.

"All babies are at first," said Tacy. "They get pretty after a while."

"My mamma seems to think it's pretty right now," Betsy said.

"Of course," said Tacy. "Mammas always do."

"Julia," said Betsy slowly, "didn't mind at all. She liked the baby right away."

"Well, but she's the oldest," said Tacy. "The oldest is always different."

Betsy rubbed her fists into her eyes to dry them. She leaned back against Tacy's arm and smelled the smell of the barn.

All of a sudden she thought how odd it was that Tacy should be talking like this. Usually she herself did most of the talking. But now Tacy was doing the talking. She was trying to comfort Betsy just as Betsy had comforted her after little Bee died. And she *had* comforted her. All the sore hurt feeling was gone.

"I'll help you wheel that baby out in the carriage," Tacy said. "We'll wheel her to the chocolate-colored house."

Betsy sat up happily. "That will be fun," she said. "And my papa said that Julia and I could name her."

"Name the baby?" cried Tacy.

"That's what he said," said Betsy proudly.

"Why, I never named a baby in my life!" said Tacy. "What will you name her?" she asked.

Betsy thought a moment. "Rosy would be a nice name," she said. "Come on, let's find Papa and tell him."

So Betsy and Tacy took hold of hands and skipped down to the house.

Mr. Ray was looking for Betsy. "I was wondering where you had gone to," he said. "Come on in, we've got to name the baby."

"Tacy and I have thought of a name. It's Rosy," Betsy said.

"Rosy!" said Betsy's father. "Rosy! It's certainly a beautiful name."

And later he and Betsy and Julia sat down in the kitchen. They drew their chairs into a circle and talked importantly in whispers. But the baby wasn't named Rosy after all. For Julia wanted to call her Ginivra.

Betsy wouldn't have Ginivra, and Julia wouldn't have Rosy. Julia wouldn't have Rosy Ginivra, and Betsy wouldn't have Ginivra Rosy.

"See here," said Betsy's father. "How about Margaret?"

Betsy liked Margaret better than Rosy. Julia liked Margaret better than Ginivra. They all thought that Margaret was a beautiful name. So they named the baby Margaret.

And Tacy was right about the baby getting pretty. She grew prettier every day.

13
Mrs. Muller Comes to Call

SOON AFTER Baby Margaret was born, two things happened to Betsy and Tacy. The first one was: they climbed the Big Hill, all the way to the white house which stood on the top. The second one was: . . . well, that comes after the first.

It was a late summer day. Goldenrod and asters were coloring the hill. The days were growing short, the birds were gathering in flocks, and there was a feeling in the air that school would be starting soon.

Betsy and Tacy were sitting in the backyard maple, and suddenly Betsy said, "Let's climb the Big Hill, all the way to the top."

"Let's," Tacy said.

So they ran and asked their mothers.

"All right," said Betsy's mother. "But you'd better take a picnic."

"All right," said Tacy's mother. "What a good thing it is that I was just baking a cake!"

So they took along a picnic. And this was the first time that they had taken a picnic in a basket. They packed their picnic in a brown wicker basket, and they both took hold of the handle, and they climbed the Big Hill.

They climbed to the ridge where wild roses grew in June. They had gone that far before. They passed the tree where they had left the egg for Bee in a nest at the very top. They passed the thorn apple tree where they had planned to make a house. There was a pasture on one side, and a cow and a calf were in that pasture; on the other side the country was open and free. They turned to look back, there, but they kept on climbing. They climbed and they climbed, and they came to the top of the hill.

The land was as flat as a plate, and there were oak trees scattered about, and the white house stood there . . . the one the sun came up behind in the morning. They went to the white house and they peeked all around it. They almost expected to find the sun in a pocket behind that house. But there was only a deep ravine, with the sound of water gurgling, and another hill beyond.

"Goodness!" said Betsy. "The world is big."

They had thought they would be satisfied when once they had climbed the Big Hill. But now they wanted to go down in the ravine, and see this water which sounded so merry, and climb the next hill.

"We will some day, too," Betsy said.

But they thought that for one day they had done enough. So they sat down on the rim of the Big Hill and ate their lunch.

They sat on the rim overlooking Hill Street. And they could look down, along the road they had come, into the maples of Hill Street and down on the roofs of their homes. They could see the trees in the vacant lot. They could see the tower of the chocolate-colored house. They could see the red brick schoolhouse where they went to school.

And they could see farther than that for they could see down to Front Street, where Tacy's father had his office and Betsy's father his store. They could see the towering chimneys of the Big Mill where the whistles blew for morning, noon and night. They could see Page Park with the white fence around it. And beyond that, down in the valley, they could see a silver ribbon. They knew that was the river.

"Mercy!" said Tacy. "There are lots of places to go."

They ate their sandwiches and the cake Tacy's mother had made and started down the hill.

And when they reached Betsy's house a great surprise awaited them. Betsy's mother was sitting on the porch, rocking the baby. She was laughing, and she looked very young and pretty, with her red hair (like Tacy's) flying around her face and the baby in her arms.

"You two little rascals, come here!" she said.

Betsy and Tacy came there.

"Do you remember the day I let you take my cardcase?" Betsy's mother asked.

Betsy and Tacy nodded. Of course they remembered.

"Well, what do you mean by leaving my cards at strange houses?"

"Strange houses?" asked Betsy.

"The houses of people we don't know."

As Betsy and Tacy did not answer, she went on: "You must have left a card at that big new house on the corner of Pleasant Street."

"Why, yes," said Betsy. "We did." But she wondered how her mother knew. She and Tacy had kept that visit a secret.

"The people had gone away," Tacy said. But she didn't say where.

"Well, here is what happened," said Mrs. Ray, still laughing. And Julia and Katie, who were standing by the porch, laughed too.

"This afternoon I was sitting here on the porch, and a carriage drove up. A lady got out, and she came up the steps of the porch and said, 'Mrs. Ray? I am Mrs. Muller. It was so kind of you to call.' And then she explained that she and her husband had moved here from Milwaukee. They had bought that house and settled it, she said, and then they had gone back to Milwaukee. But now they have come here to stay and get their little girl in school."

"Their little girl!" cried Betsy and Tacy together. "Is there a little girl?"

"Of course. Didn't I tell you that the little girl was with her? Julia and Katie entertained her, for I couldn't find you two. But she's just about your age."

"What's she like?" asked Betsy and Tacy breathlessly.

"Oh, she's darling," said Julia and Katie. "She's perfectly sweet."

"She has little yellow curls," said Julia. "Short ones. Like this."

"And big blue eyes," said Katie.

"She wore the prettiest dress," said Julia. "White lace with bows of blue ribbon all over."

"And she dances," said Katie. "She danced for us. All by herself."

Betsy and Tacy looked at each other.

"What's her name?" asked Betsy.

"Her name is Tib." "It's short for Thelma." Julia and Katie explained.

Betsy and Tacy didn't say a word. They started down Hill Street. "Do you suppose we'll like her?" they asked . . . but silently. Down in their hearts they thought they wouldn't.

They took hold of hands when they reached the vacant lot. They walked as though they were walking into danger. The tall trees and the bushes and the brush seemed to wait in breathless excitement as Betsy and Tacy approached the chocolate-colored house.

14
Tib

THEY APPROACHED the chocolate-colored house from the rear for it faced on Pleasant Street. On the back lawn was an oak tree which stood on a small knoll. On the knoll they saw what looked like a clothes pin, standing prongs up. It was a little girl standing on her head.

She righted herself when they came near and stood on her bare feet. She was dainty and small.

Her arms, legs and face were tanned, which made her blue eyes look even bluer than they were and her short fluff of yellow hair look very yellow. She stared at them silently out of her round blue eyes.

"What were you doing?" asked Betsy.

"Standing on my head."

"What were you doing that for?"

"I was practicing."

"It must be hard," said Betsy.

"Oh, no, it isn't." The little girl looked surprised. Tacy didn't say a word. She was bashful.

Betsy stared back at the little girl. It was certainly Tib. "But my sister said you had a white lace dress on," she said at last.

"I took it off when I came home," Tib answered. "I'm not allowed to play in my best dress."

"Neither am I," said Betsy. "Neither is Tacy. I wish we could see your dress, though," she added after a moment.

"Do you?" asked Tib, looking surprised again. "I'll show it to you."

She led the way into the chocolate-colored house.

They went in by the back door. "Wipe your feet," said Tib, pausing on the doormat. The kitchen was so clean . . . it shone like a polished pan. It smelled good, of something baking. A hired girl was standing by the stove.

There was a swinging door which led into the dining room and another door which led into a pantry full of glittery china and glass. The third door led up some narrow stairs and up these they followed Tib.

Upstairs was a long hall with doors admitting to the bedrooms.

Tib took them into one of these, and hanging in a closet was the white lace dress.

"It's a beautiful dress," said Betsy.

Tacy touched one of the pale blue satin bows.

Tib led them down the hall. There were front stairs as well

as back stairs! They went down the front stairs, and just as the steps turned at a little landing, they came in view of the pane of colored glass. The afternoon sunlight, streaming through it, turned it to ruby red.

"Tacy and I like that colored glass," said Betsy.

"What colored glass?" asked Tib.

"That colored glass over your door."

"Do you. Why?" asked Tib. She looked at it as though she had never noticed it before.

"We like your tower too," said Betsy.

"What tower?" asked Tib. "Do you mean the round room? That's our front parlor."

They crossed the hall and entered it.

It was round and beautiful. Hanging over the piano was a picture of an old man giving a little girl a music lesson. The chairs and sofa were covered with blue velvet and there was a bamboo table draped with a blue silk scarf. The table held two little china dolls, a shepherd and a shepherdess.

Tib led them through blue velvet curtains into the back parlor. This had a window seat from which you could see the red brick schoolhouse. A lady sat there sewing. She was short and chunky and had yellow hair like Tib's and earrings in her ears.

"Is this the little Ray girl?" she asked.

"Yes, ma'am," answered Betsy. "I'm Betsy and this is Tacy."

Tacy held her head down and covered her face with her curls.

"Well, I hope you children will all be good friends," Tib's mother said, smiling.

"Mamma," said Tib. "May we have some coffee cake?"

"Yes," said the lady. "Matilda will give you some. But eat it out on the knoll."

So Matilda—she was the hired girl—gave them some coffee cake. It was hot out of the oven. And they sat down to eat it on the knoll.

Tib kept staring at Betsy and Tacy with her round blue eyes. She looked awed and admiring, which was nice but very strange. For Tib was the one who danced, thought Betsy. She was the one who had a white lace dress. She was the one who had a house with front and back stairs and a tower and a pane of colored glass.

Betsy and Tacy looked at each other. Both of them looked surprised. They hadn't expected to like her, but they did.

Tib didn't say a word and neither did Tacy, so at last Betsy said:

"When you came to our house, we were up on the Big Hill."

"Were you?" asked Tib.

"We climbed to the very top," said Betsy.

"Did you?" Tib replied.

"There's a little hill too," said Betsy. "With a bench on it. We eat our supper there."

"All by yourselves?" asked Tib.

"All by ourselves," said Betsy.

"And Betsy makes up stories," said Tacy. It was the first word she had said.

"Do you mean," asked Tib, "that she tells about Cinderella?"

"No, I make them up," said Betsy.

"But how can you?" Tib asked.

"Why, I just do," said Betsy. "Tacy helps me."

"Will you make one up now?" asked Tib.

"Yes, if you want me to. I'll make one up about you and me and Tacy and that pane of colored glass over your door."

Tib was speechless with astonishment, but Tacy jumped to her feet and said:

"Let's go up to our bench. That's the best place for stories."

So she took one of Tib's hands and Betsy took the other. And they walked through the vacant lot and up Hill Street Hill.

As they walked they were very busy talking.

"We've got a piano box we play in," Betsy said.

"And Betsy's got a baby sister," Tacy said.

"We play paper dolls," said Betsy.

"And store," said Tacy.

"We dress up and go calling."

"And Betsy makes up games."

Tib held their hands tightly. She sighed deeply with content.

"I'm glad I came here," she said. "I like this better than Milwaukee."

Betsy and Tacy stopped still. They looked at each other, their eyes as round as Tib's. She liked Hill Street better than Milwaukee! Well, they had always known it was nice.

After a silent moment they went slowly on toward the bench on the hill.

"We'll have lots of fun," said Betsy. "You and me and Tacy. Lots of things will happen."

And so they did.

THE END

Maud Hart Lovelace and Her World

Maud Palmer Hart circa 1906

Collection of Sharla Scannell Whalen

MAUD HART LOVELACE was born on April 25, 1892, in Mankato, Minnesota. Like Betsy, Maud followed her mother around the house at age five asking questions such as "How do you spell 'going down the street'?" for the stories she had already begun to write. Soon she was writing poems and plays. When Maud was ten, a booklet of her poems was printed; and by age eighteen, she had sold her first short story.

The Hart family left Mankato shortly after Maud's high school graduation in 1910 and settled in Minneapolis, where Maud attended the University of Minnesota. In 1917, she married Delos W. Lovelace, a newspaper reporter who later became a popular writer of short stories.

The Lovelaces' daughter, Merian, was born in 1931. Maud would tell her daughter bedtime stories about her childhood, and it was these stories that gave her the idea of writing the Betsy-Tacy books. Maud did not intend to write an entire series when *Betsy-Tacy*, the first book, was published in 1940, but readers asked for more stories. So Maud took Betsy through high school and beyond college to the "great world" and marriage. The final book in the series, *Betsy's Wedding*, was published in 1955.

The Betsy-Tacy books are based very closely on Maud's own life. "I could make it all up, but in these Betsy-Tacy stories, I love to work from real incidents," Maud wrote. "The Ray family is a true portrayal of the Hart family. Mr. Ray is like Tom Hart; Mrs. Ray like Stella Palmer Hart; Julia like Kathleen; Margaret like Helen; and Betsy is like me, except that, of course, I glamorized her to make her a proper heroine." Tacy and Tib are based on Maud's real-life best friends, Frances "Bick" Kenney and Marjorie "Midge" Gerlach, and Deep Valley is based on Mankato.

In fact, so much in the books was taken from real life that it is sometimes difficult to draw the line between fact and fiction. And through the years, Maud received a great deal of fan mail from readers who were fascinated by the question—what is true, and what is made up?

About Betsy-Tacy

IN THE SPRING OF 1897, Maud Hart and Frances "Bick" Kenney met at Maud's fifth birthday party and became lifelong friends—just like Betsy and Tacy. As Maud wrote to Bick Kenney's granddaughter in 1960, when she was sixty-eight years old, "Tacy certainly is your red-haired grandmother and has been my dearest friend ever since my fifth birthday."

In the story, Betsy thinks Tacy is calling names when she first introduces herself because her name is so unusual. (Maud first discovered the name "Tacy" in a colonial newspaper when she was doing research for another book.) We don't know if this happened in real life, but it's possible that a similar misunderstanding resulted when Bick told Maud *her* name, which is also a bit unusual. Bick Kenney's niece explained the origin of the nickname: "Frances Kenney had very red hair as a child and was called 'Brick.' Not being old enough to pronounce it properly, she called herself 'Bick.'" And Bick is the name she used throughout her life.

Maud seemed to recall the occasion of her fifth birthday very vividly, and much of the description

Maud's straight hair was curled for these photographs, taken for the occasion of her fifth birthday.

Lois Lenski probably referred to the photos when she drew Betsy in her special party dress.

of the party in the book was based on her memories. For example, she remembered that she wore a "checked silk [dress] in tan, rose, and cream," like Betsy's. And Bick really did bring Maud a little glass pitcher as a birthday gift. Although its gold-painted rim has now worn away, the pitcher can be seen today in the Maud Hart Lovelace wing of the Minnesota Valley Regional Library in Mankato, Minnesota.

In fact, Betsy and Tacy's adventures throughout the book are based on Maud's real childhood experiences. In an interview, Maud described some of the games she and Bick used to play, which will sound very familiar: "We used to color sand and put it in bottles and have sand stores and sell it. We cut our paper dolls out of the magazines. We dressed up in our mothers' long skirts. We went on picnics."

In 1897, there really was a bench on the hill at the top of the street where Maud and Bick ate their suppers, although it was gone by 1906 or 1907. But readers may be pleased to know that a memorial bench was placed there in 1989, and it is still there today—a testimony to the powerful effect of Maud's writing, and in commemoration of a very special friendship.

Maud (right) and Bick (left) were lifelong friends— here they are at age ten.

The glass pitcher that Bick gave to Maud for her fifth birthday is now on display at the public library in Mankato.

Maud lived with her family in this little house at 333 Center Street.

The Ray house, at 333 Hill Street, closely resembles Maud's.

Maud's mother, Stella Palmer Hart, was a schoolteacher before her marriage to Tom Hart.

In this photo, Kathleen Hart, Maud's older sister and the model for Julia Ray, is about eight years old.

Maud and her friends attended Pleasant Grove School, a redbrick building that was built in 1871.

Lois Lenski's drawing of the schoolhouse.

Maud once spoke of "the fresh exciting world in which children live" and said, "I do think I remember that better than most grown-ups." Many generations of Betsy-Tacy fans would certainly agree!

Maud Hart Lovelace died on March 11, 1980. But her legacy lives on in the beloved series she created and in her legions of fans, many of whom are members of the Betsy-Tacy Society and the Maud Hart Lovelace Society. For more information, write to:

The Betsy-Tacy Society
P.O. Box 94
Mankato, MN 56002-0094
(507) 345-9777
www.betsy-tacysociety.org

The Maud Hart Lovelace Society
Fifty 94th Circle NW, # 201
Minneapolis, MN 55448

Adapted from *The Betsy-Tacy Companion: A Biography of Maud Hart Lovelace* by Sharla Scannell Whalen

This map of the Hill Street neighborhood by Lois Lenski was printed on the endpapers of early editions of the first four Betsy-Tacy books.